CW01210523

scuffed granny

Short Stories for Open Minds

By Mark A. Gagnon

This is a work of fiction. Names, characters, places, and incidents are products of the author's imagination or are used fictitiously. Any resemblance to actual events or locales or persons, living or dead, is entirely coincidental.

Short Stories for Open Minds: Copyright © 2019 by Mark A. Gagnon. All rights reserved. Except as permitted under U.S. Copyright Act of 1976, no part of this book may be reproduced, stored in a retrievable system, or transmitted by any means without written permission from the author.

ISBN: 9781690606482

Acknowledgements

Special thanks to my wife Linda for her support. I never would have pursued this endeavor without her.

Also, thanks to my fellow members of Pelican Pens for their encouragement, and to Judy Loose of Loose Links for her editing expertise.

Contents

Click on Accept 1

Revelation 7

Carpe Diem 13

Gone Phishing 17

Reality Check 21

The Road to Understanding 23

    (Thirty Years Later) 26

Rat Trap 29

Ring Around the Rosie 39

No Respect 45

Survival Sense 47

The Gift of Time 51

    1349 53

    The Present 57

    1362 59

    1366 60

    1461 62

    1658 65

    The Present 68

    1815 70

The Present	71
Ice and Fire	75
Glimpse into the Future	81
One Man's Trash…	85
Happy Birthday Mikey	89
Under Pressure	95
Tick…Tick…Tick	101
Damn Liberals	105
Stan's Reality — Altered	111
Mirror Image	117
Cryptogram	125
The Good Deed	129
Just Enough Time	135
XXI	139

Click on Accept

It was one of those nights—nothing on TV and too early to go to bed—so I went web surfing. I'd heard about a site that was similar to Amazon, but all their items were pre-owned (used). They sold everything from houses to hose clamps, vacation packages to vacuums, you name it they had it for sale. I eventually found the site and started exploring a virtual cornucopia of items. Why someone would buy slightly used shoelaces is beyond me, but there they were for 25 cents per lace.

As I was scanning, an information box popped up on my screen informing me that, after reading the Terms and Conditions, I would need to click the **Accept** button if I wanted to continue using the site. I had 10 seconds to click **Accept**. No one, me included, ever takes the time to read the 25 or so pages of legalese in the conditions box. I clicked

Accept and continued browsing. About an hour later, I called it a night and went to bed.

The next morning started as usual. I donned my workout gear and headed out for my morning run. As soon as I stepped through the door, I saw it, an empty driveway where my car should have been parked. Someone had stolen my car! I was about to head back inside and call the police when I heard my neighbor call, "What's wrong with your car? I saw a tow truck take it away early this morning."

"What company?" I asked. He didn't get the name, but as there are only two towing companies in town, it wouldn't be difficult to trace my car's location. With a 50/50 chance of getting the right company, I dialed the first number. Things were looking up; they had my car. I told them I would be there ASAP to reclaim it. When I asked who arranged for the tow, I was told it was the Accept Corporation. I responded that I had never heard of them, but would be there later to reclaim my car.

Feeling a little better about my car's whereabouts, I decided to have breakfast and shower before calling a friend for a ride to the salvage yard. Shower complete, I grabbed a towel to dry off and heard voices in the hallway. Figuring it must be the clock radio, I stepped out of the bathroom directly in front of a middle-aged woman with a young couple in tow.

The screams of startled surprise finally subsided as I wrapped the towel around my waist while asking, "Who the hell are you people, and why are you in my house?"

The middle-aged woman blurted out while brandishing a piece of paper as if warding off evil spirits, "I'm with RE/MAX, and this house is listed for sale by the Accept Corporation. You're not supposed to be here."

I explained to the trio that I never listed my house for sale; there had been a major screw up. I asked them to leave so I could get dressed and get this all straightened out.

The woman left in a huff along with her charges. The younger woman looked back over her shoulder, gave me the once over and smiled. No time for that nonsense, I had to do some serious research. My computer wasn't working, and neither was my cell phone, which meant I had to ask a neighbor for a ride to the library to use the public computers and payphone. After 10 minutes online, I was able to locate a phone number for the Accept Corporation. I went to the payphone, dropped in some coins and dialed. An electronic voice answered and informed me there was a 30-minute wait time, and promptly switched on heavy metal music.

I returned to the computer more determined than ever to find a way to undo this mess. Back on Accept's website, I used my customer password from the previous night and accessed the Terms and Conditions I had ignored. There on page 21, paragraphs 3 thru 5, everything that was happening was clearly spelled out. By clicking the **Accept** button, I had ceded to the Accept Corporation all deeds and titles of properties and possessions in my name that they chose to take both now and in the future. By ignoring my responsibility to do due diligence, I had given away all my property. This is how Accept acquired its inventory of preowned items.

As I stared blankly at the screen feeling despondent, another information box appeared.

*Should you wish to cancel your agreement with The Accept Corporation, you must click the **Accept** button. We are giving you this one-time opportunity to purchase all your former belongings at market value plus a 15% handling charge. There is also a 10% inventory adjustment fee. You have 10 seconds to click the button starting now.*

Mark A. Gagnon

Revelation

I can't remember a time when Maddie wasn't in my life. We met as toddlers, our parents were next-door neighbors, and we spent almost every day playing together. Many children drift apart once they start school, but not Maddie and me. We attended the same grammar school, had the same teachers, and helped each other with homework. Inseparable, joined at the hip, two peas in a pod, and all those other tired clichés were used to describe us by the adults. That's how it was right up to the day her father got promoted, and the family moved to another state.

We would write from time to time, send Christmas and birthday cards, but when you're a ten-year-old boy, too many other things compete for your time. The families would visit on rare occasions, and Maddie and I would pick up as if we'd never been apart. This long-distance relationship continued through high school. During my junior year I applied to and was accepted at several universities. I didn't deliberate a lot on school choice; I picked the one with a strong robotics curriculum. You can imagine my surprise when I called Maddie to share my good news only to hear she was going to attend the same university.

Earth's population was shrinking at an alarming rate due to global warming and the various exotic diseases created by it. Only one couple in a thousand was able to conceive, and out of that group only one in a hundred produced a fully developed child. This was the reason that the robotics field was in such high demand. Someone or something had to do the work.

We quickly fell back into our old habits. Not only did we study together, we never seemed to be apart. Although we both worked in robotics, Maddie's specialty was designing, upgrading, and programing the positronic brain. Mine was improving the physical platform based on the human form.

It came as no surprise to anyone that one week after graduation, we married. A robotics firm hired us as a team to continue improving their product line. Unfortunately, children were impossible for us, but that didn't matter. We had each other, and our new creations became our children. This was our life, and it lasted mostly unaltered for fifty years.

We can ignore change when it happens subtly, especially if it causes negative things to affect the one you love. I always felt that Maddie was my intellectual superior, but she began forgetting conversations and where she had placed items. Sometimes she even forgot the name of the town where we grew up. I couldn't ignore the signs any longer and convinced her to visit the company doctor. In today's world, corporations provide healthcare for all their employees at no charge; it's considered the cost of doing business. The doctors put Maddie through a battery of tests, and we waited in the reception room for the results. The VP of Engineering entered the room and asked if we would join him in his office. He was not the person I expected to speak with, but I remained quiet until I had all the facts. He began by telling us how proud he was of both of us and our accomplishments in the robotics field. I thanked him for his kind words but didn't want any further delays.

"What's wrong with my wife?" I blurted out.

"Stated simply, her positronic brain is quickly coming to the end of its life."

This man was an idiot! I was about to tell him so when he raised his hands in a defensive gesture and said, "Please let me explain. You and Maddie are prototypes my predecessors created more than seventy-five years ago. The idea was to create robots that believed they were human in every way possible. From time to time we would add enhancements, tweak physical and psychological behaviors, and whatever else we deemed necessary. The two of you, along with the work you've done in the field, have allowed us to create a superior product. You should be proud of your contributions."

"You can't expect me to accept that explanation. Everyone knows that the android robot is created in full adult form because it's impossible to grow one starting as an infant and morphing it into a grownup. I have vivid memories of a happy and rich childhood, and those memories include Maddie."

"You have those memories because my predecessors took episodes from television shows like *The Brady Bunch* and *Leave It to Beaver* along with several others and modified them to create the ideal childhood. Your childhood! Then they downloaded them into your memory. Your college memories are real because that's when you both started interacting with humans. You and Maddie are this company's greatest achievement."

I took Maddie's hand and in a quiet voice told her we were leaving. I then turned to the VP of Engineering and asked, "What is your definition of being human? Is it simply flesh and bones, or is there more? If your answer includes compassion, love, intellect, a sense of family, the ability to connect with others, and so much more, then you have just described Maddie and me. Our physical bodies may be comprised of composites and silicates, but our identities are as individual and real as any other person. We are more than complex machines, we exist!"

With that, Maddie and I left for home to contemplate the rest of our lives together, however long or short that may be.

Carpe Diem

Ronald sat in his cubical, which was identical to 150 others, staring at a banner 8' long by 3' tall suspended over the supervisor's desk. Printed in thick bold letters it read, "SEIZE THE DAY." He had stared at the sign for the past five months while making call after call, from endless lists of phone numbers, trying to sell complete strangers extended warranty programs for their cars. After each call, he added a notation: no answer; no longer owns the car; not interested; please remove from list; and occasionally, sold. The sold annotation was rare and a cause for a mini-celebration. Once he'd called all the numbers, he would walk to the supervisor's desk, turn in the names, and receive a new file.

This workday started like all the others with Ronald staring at the banner, translated from the Latin, "Carpe Diem," a phrase first penned by Horace, the Roman philosopher, over 2,000 years ago. The problem was Horace never included instructions on how to seize the day. Some advice was as good as no advice at all. *Today will be different*, thought Ronald. *I spent four years as an undergraduate plus another year obtaining my Master's, and I can do better than this.*

Ronald made up his mind. He would finish his list, take it to the supervisor, repeat the lyrics from an old country classic "Take this Job and Shove It," and walk out a free man. He would seize the day and find a new path to travel, one that didn't include call centers.

With the final number on his current list called and annotated, Ronald rose from his desk ready to stride forward toward the unknown. Before he could take the first step on his thousand-mile journey, his cell phone rang.

"Hello, this is Ronald."

"Sir, I'm calling about your student loan. When can we expect the next payment?"

"I get paid this Thursday. I'll have it in the mail on Friday."

"Thank you, Ronald. I'll make a note to that effect by your name. Have a blessed day."

Ronald replaced the phone in his pocket, picked up the completed list, and walked to the supervisor's desk. He accepted a new file of names and numbers and returned to his cubical. Once again, the day had seized him.

Mark A. Gagnon

Gone Phishing

I awoke to another beautiful and hopefully profitable day by my alarm clock playing the old Louis Armstrong ditty, "Gone fishin' instead of just a wishin'." It's surprising that a song written so many years ago can be relevant today to a person in my line of work. I know what some of you must be thinking, "Work! How can you possibly call scamming people out of their life savings work? All you do is send out an email blast, and the computer does the rest."

True, what I do isn't rocket science. Greed, guilt, and fear are the tools I use against my marks. I admit, in the beginning getting people to part with their cash was much easier. It simply involved sending out a personalized email explaining that the target had just inherited a large amount of money from a distant relative. They only needed to send enough cash via Western Union to cover the taxes, and the windfall was theirs. In the beginning

I received money on a daily basis, sent by the greedy would-be inheritors anxious to collect funds from someone they'd never met. Then the Nigerians started the African Prince con, which was so blatantly ridiculous that people became cautious. The river of dollars slowed to a trickle, and it was back to the drawing board.

My next venture into parting people from their savings was the bogus IRS phone call. Everyone cheats on their taxes to some degree, so playing on a person's guilty conscious was almost too easy. Spoof a phone number, use a digital voice, and people are convinced big brother has them cold. All good things come to an end, and once the news media sounded the alarm, most people just hung up the phone.

Generating fear is what my current endeavor is all about. I start the email with an official-looking bank logo followed by a message telling the recipient that their account has been locked due to an attempted hack. I ask the mark to provide their social security number and password to assist fraud protection in verifying their identity. Never checking to see if the account is locked, people gratefully provide the requested information. Now I have options. I can either empty the account myself—a task that has some risk involved—or I can sell the data on the dark web to the highest bidder.

My next sting is almost complete. It is a masterpiece, a work of genius if I do say so myself.

"What is it?" you ask. You'll need to figure it out for yourself. Yes, it's a great day to go phishing!

Mark A. Gagnon

Reality Check

Now that was a well-deserved weekend off! My back and legs were killing me, not to mention my arms felt like they were about to fall off. Yes, I needed this long weekend to try and pull myself back together. All the stress and strain that comes with my job would cause someone made of lesser quality material to give up and collapse in a heap.

When I was created, I knew I was destined for greatness. Why wouldn't I think that; I was a special order after all. The material used in my construction was all heavy-duty: reinforced gussets; extra-thick vinyl at all the wear points; closed-cell foam, and top-quality brass fasteners. With a design like this, I knew I was bound for the White House, Supreme Court, or at least the Governor's Mansion. Yes, I knew I was headed for the big time. My assembly complete, the shipping department lovingly placed me in my well-padded secure crate for transport.

Reality is a cruel mistress. After being carefully uncrated, I was placed where everyone could see me in keeping with my superior pedigree, or so I thought. But what was this somewhat crowded room? The door opened, and a rather rotund person walked through. As the door gently closed, controlled by the attached hydraulic mechanism, I was able to read the nameplate that was proudly displayed.

Dr. John Shultz, M.D.
Bariatric Surgery and Weight Loss Clinic

Now I get it! My sturdy build wasn't done for posterity, but for large posteriors. I hadn't realized, greatness comes in many forms.

The Road to Understanding

Clip... Clop... Clip... Clop...

A father and son road atop a horse-drawn cart on the way to the seaside village to sell the family wares. The clear day revealed gently rolling hills divided by stone walls and a view across the gulf to the mainland.

"Dad?"

"Yes, Son."

"Who made those stone walls, and why are there so many?"

"Our ancestors made the walls when they first came to the island."

"Ant-sisters, that's a funny name. Have I ever met one?"

"It's an-ces-tors, and yes, you have. Mom and I are your ancestors, so are both Grandads and Grandmas, and their parents, and all the people way back to the settlers who first came to our island. It took all those people to make you, and if you have children, you'll be one of their ancestors."

"I get it, I think. But why did they make those walls?"

"Well, Son, there are two reasons. First, the soil here is rocky and needed to be cleared of stones so people could plant crops. They then used the rocks to build walls. Second, our ancestors wanted walls to keep their livestock contained on their property and for protection from their neighbors. Building walls started on the continent, where people had wars and disagreements. Even though they came to the island to escape war and strife, our forefathers felt things might not be different here, so they prepared for the worst."

"Dad, what's war? It sounds like a bad thing. We won't have one here, will we? I mean, what makes war happen?"

"Those are hard questions to answer, Son. I hope we'll never see a war here. The people who live on the island may not always agree with each other, but they put the welfare of the islanders first."

The father pointed to the hazy land showing across the water. "Over there are many, many more people. They tend to be more concerned about what's best for themselves and their own beliefs rather than what's best for the population as a whole. On the continent, there are things called countries. People in one country may speak a different language and have different beliefs than the people in neighboring countries. The citizens of one country may feel the best way to preserve their way of life is to wage war on their neighbors. By eliminating or controlling those other countries, they believe they can achieve lasting peace. Unfortunately, history has shown, over and over again, that war isn't the solution."

"How big is the continent, Dad? If all those people live on it, it must be huge! Have you ever gone there?"

"Yes, I've been there, and yes, it is huge. If you started walking from one shore, it would take you three months to reach the other shore."

"Wow! I want to go there someday, Dad. I bet I can make them stop making war. Will you take me?

"No, Son, I won't take you. Someday, if you want to go, you'll need to make that trip on your own. As for today, this is your first of many trips to the port to learn the family business."

"Thanks for taking me with you today, Dad. I love you!

(Thirty Years Later)

Clip…Clop…Clip… Clop

"Dad, this place is still as beautiful as the day I left it for the mainland."

"Well, Son, not much changes here. Old Bess died a few years ago, so we had to buy a new horse, and the wagon needed some repairs, but that's about it. Of course, with my various ailments, I don't make the trip to town anymore. One of the neighbors usually handles the port trips for me."

Father and son again rode atop the horse-drawn cart to sell wares at the port.

"Son?"

"Yes, Dad."

"Did you find what you were looking for on the continent?

"I did, Dad. I traveled from one end to the other and back again. I met different peoples and experienced many cultures. Everywhere I went, I described this island and told them how we've avoided war. I tried to demonstrate the benefits of working together and putting aside prejudices. Some refused to listen and called me a subversive. Others did listen and attempted to implement change, but they usually failed. Overall, I think I did as much as one man can. I realized after all my traveling that what I was looking for is right here, on this cart, taking care of the family business with you."

"Thanks for taking me with you today, Son. I love you."

"I love you too, Dad."

Rat Trap

Most people find rats unsettling, and Julian was no exception. After being forced to deal with one rat in particular, he now fears them.

Julian Hawk is a successful writer; not in the Michael Connelly or Lee Child category of successful, but he has sold three books with a contract from a major publisher for more. The twist in his stories is that the bad guy always gets away. There is no Jack Reacher or Harry Bosch to somehow save the day and put things right. His fan base seems to like it when the smart criminal wins.

With fame comes distraction and less time to develop a new story. So far, Julian's written about a jewelry heist, a Ponzi scheme, and an arms dealer. The easy path is to revive one of the existing characters and continue that character's journey. That was what Julian had planned to do until he received a bizarre letter. The correspondence was typed on old-style onion skin paper with what appeared to be a manual typewriter. Even stranger was that it was sent to his house and not the P.O. Box that his publicist had set up to divert fan mail, and it had no postmark. The most disturbing thing was the letter's content.

> Julian,
>
> I need your help. In four days, I will steal the contents of a safe located on the private yacht "*North Star*" while it's moored at Skyport Marina on New York's East River. You need not know what I'm taking or how I've obtained my information. What I need from you is the perfect plan. I'll be in touch soon with more detail.
>
> By the way, I've tapped your phones, and your movements are being monitored. Any attempt at notifying the authorities will result in the death of someone close to you.

```
I'm        looking       forward     to      our
collaboration.
```

The Rat

Julian re-read the letter three times before placing it on the side table next to his chair. *What a sick joke. This has got to be the work of Willy. He's always trying, sometimes successfully, to get one over on me.*

He picked up the phone and called Willy, his old Air Force buddy. "Okay, smartass, what's with the creepy letter, and where did you find the antique typewriter?"

"I haven't got a clue what you're talking about, Julian. You need to explain."

Before Julian could say another word, a text message popped up on his phone's screen which read, *Hang up the phone now!*

"My bad, Willy. I hit the wrong speed dial number. Got to go." Julian hung up the phone with trembling hands.

Two seconds later, his phone buzzed. With a shaky voice he answered, "Hello?"

An electronically altered voice said, "I'll give you that one, but that's it. From now on any mention of our little project, and someone dies."

"Okay, this is crazy!" Julian blurted out. "If you can do all this surveillance stuff, and you have the information you need about the boat and the safe, why do you need me?"

"Simple, I'm your biggest fan. I want to see if you're as good as you think you are. Better get busy. I need to be out of New York and in Washington D.C. for another engagement late the day after the heist." The phone went dead, and Julian's heart skipped a couple of beats.

Although his fear was stronger than before, Julian began to think of this as a challenge, both to his skill as a writer and his acumen for working through a problem to a satisfactory resolution. The Rat would get his fool-proof plan, and Julian would figure out how to catch this Rat and protect his friends.

Research is what makes an okay story a great story. The devil is in the details, and all those other clichés, are right on the money. Julian spent the next two days learning everything he could about the marina—its security and evening activities. He researched the least conspicuous way out of NYC and the best way to arrive in D.C. unnoticed.

Julian also had a regular schedule to maintain. The Rat couldn't expect him to stop associating with friends, going to book signings, and just plain living his life. During a social function, Julian ran into retired FBI agent, Mike Jones, whom he'd used as a consultant for one of his books. Could he trust this man? Never having seen the Rat, Julian knew he could be anyone. Suddenly his phone buzzed! *Stay away from the FBI guy. I'm watching!*

Unnerved, Julian looked around the room at people talking in small groups and at security cameras. Julian expected he would be watched and had prepared for it. He joined a group of people closest to him and clumsily spilled his drink on a friend. While profusely apologizing and dabbing at her damp sleeve, Julian palmed a note into her hand that he'd written before coming to the function. With his back to the closest surveillance camera Julian whispered, "Before you leave, give this to Mike Jones. You know him. It's very important, and don't be obvious giving it to him. This is no joke!"

At home later that night, his phone rang. Before Julian could say hello, the electronic voice said, "What do you have for me?"

"Okay, here's what I've worked out." Julian tried to sound confident. "Every Tuesday evening at 7:30 p.m. there's a booze cruise that leaves from Skyport Marina, two slips away from the *North Star*. Buy a ticket online for tomorrow night. Take the cruise, be seen, and enjoy yourself. The ship returns at 10:00 p.m. You want to be one of the first people to disembark. Casually wander over to the *North Star*. You should have approximately 10 minutes to board, crack the safe, and return to the unloading area where you can hail a cab to the Port Authority Bus Terminal.

"While you're online, also purchase a one-way ticket for the Greyhound bus leaving at 1:00 a.m. for DC. The bus will make a stop at the Baltimore Greyhound terminal, which is where you'll get off. Take a taxi to Baltimore/Penn station and board a MARC light rail train for DC. The trains run about every twenty minutes starting at 4:20 a.m., so you'll have plenty of options. At this point, my job is done."

"Very good," said the voice. "I like the use of multiple modes of transportation." The connection cut off abruptly.

The Tuesday evening of the heist, Julian was signing books at a local library. An attractive woman in a pantsuit approached his table. She casually brushed back one side of her coat to discreetly reveal a badge. "I'm a friend of Mike Jones," she said. "He told me to ask you for a signed copy of your first book."

"Any friend of Mike's is a friend of mine," said Julian and handed her the book. "Tell Mike the most interesting part is chapter three." The woman smiled, thanked Julian and walked out. What he had slipped into chapter three of the book he gave the female agent was a copy of the same itinerary the thief had.

It was almost midnight by the time the FBI put together a plan to catch the thief. They didn't know what he looked like and decided it would be best to pick him up in Baltimore. Their team waited to see who left the bus and went to the train station. The plan worked, and the Baltimore agents picked up a man for questioning. He possessed nothing unusual and had a perfectly good reason for changing modes of transportation. After several hours of questioning, the police let him go. Besides, the owner of the *North Star* said nothing was missing from his safe. The agents were not happy.

Julian showed the local agents the letter and his phone with the text messages, so they knew he hadn't created this to sell more books. "It's a mystery," Julian told Mike. "I may never know what this was all about."

Later that week another letter arrived at his house.

```
Julian,
I imagine you're looking for answers
and have had little success. First,
you fulfilled your part of the deal,
so your family and friends are safe.
The item my associate took from the
safe was a thumb drive with a list of
customers the boat's owner was
selling guns to. The robbery will
never be reported. A certain African
warlord doesn't like competition and
needed the list to cull the herd, so
to speak.

I never would have considered buses,
but that worked extremely well. My
associate met me at the Port
Authority Building and passed the
drive to me while we were waiting for
our respective buses. He took the
Greyhound to DC while I took a Peter
```

Pan bus to Boston. When the Feds sprung their Rat Trap, I was already 300 miles away with the metaphoric cheese safe in hand. As in your stories, the smart criminal always gets away.

I've enjoyed working with you. We need to do it again sometime!
Regards,
The Rat

Ring Around the Rosie

Mystifying Marvin and his assistant, Bodacious Brenda, worked the senior circuit, which consisted of 55+ and assisted living communities. The duo, whose shows never lasted past 9:00 p.m., bewildered and impressed their audiences with sleight of hand and Marvin's specialty, hypnosis. Brenda meandered through the crowd selecting unsuspecting and relatively spry audience members to participate in the hypnosis segment of the act.

Marvin started with one "volunteer," placing him or her in a hypnotic state and asking that person to act out a specific scenario. The number of people on stage would grow to twenty or so. Marvin and Brenda divided the large group into smaller groups and Marvin disseminated specific instructions to each cluster. When the hypnotist said a predetermined command, the assemblage would start to mimic barnyard animals. Four or five strutted and clucked like chickens; several others began mooing like cows; still others bleated like sheep. It was all great fun, and the audience usually delivered a standing ovation. Their show performed in all the local venues, then departed for the next town.

Two days after Marvin and Brenda's departure, an armored car pulled up in front of the local bank. Two guards exited with a hand truck and entered the establishment. Per protocol, a third guard stayed in the back, protecting its valuable shipment and to reopen the vehicle's rear door when his partners emerged from the bank with their cargo.

After the guards entered the bank, a small group of elderly people began gathering by the entrance. The group grew in number until by the time the guards re-emerged, approximately thirty-five seniors meandered around aimlessly in the area between the bank and the armored truck. The guards, both in their late twenties, didn't feel threatened by a gaggle of grey-hairs and shouldered their way through the throng towards the armored car. Their partner, seeing the guards approach, opened the vehicle's door.

The guards were in the middle of the retirees when a person dressed from head to foot in loose-fitting garb and wearing a V-for-Vengeance mask, stepped from an adjacent alleyway. The person, sex undeterminable, placed a seventies-style boom box on the sidewalk and pushed the play button.

Upon hearing the song "Ring Around the Rosie" sung by a children's choir, the assembly formed a tight circle around the guards, held hands, and joined in singing the old ditty. When the lyrics "we all fall down" were sung, the crowd did exactly that. The perplexed guards were left vulnerable to a pepper-spray attack the disguised person unleashed. At the same moment and with perfect precision, an identically clad individual appeared and pepper-sprayed the remaining guard.

The song started again, and everyone stood and repeated their earlier actions. Both perpetrators entered the truck during the second chorus, ignored the cash, seized two medium-size pouches filled with precious gems, rushed to waiting motorcycles, and made their escape. Approximately 45 seconds had elapsed from the start of the robbery to the twosome's getaway.

The boom box continued to play the same song for two minutes, and then an electronically altered voice said "Go home children." The tape disintegrated in a puff of smoke. Members of the group slowly regained their composure, shocked to see the three guards writhing in pain. The police arrived and transported everyone to headquarters on a bus. Most of the seniors didn't know anyone else in the group and had no recollection of what took place. The only common thread was they all enjoyed the children's song, "Ring Around the Rosie."

Marvin and Brenda sipped drinks and enjoyed a sumptuous meal at a five-star restaurant several hundred miles from their latest escapade. Their manager/fence called and told them about a new town filled with senior communities near Toronto, and a bank that distributed gold mini-bars.

Marvin said, "I bet the Canadians will enjoy playing 'Ring Around the Rosie,' eh."

Mark A. Gagnon

No Respect

I don't get it! People are always calling me "a pain." Just what have I done to deserve such disrespect? I let in the light, block the wind and cold, and can help enhance a room's beauty. I can even protect people from flying hurricane debris. So, what is it that has garnered me this moniker? The only way I can become a pain is if someone cuts themselves on me while trying to replace me. I know a lot of people don't like cleaning me, but is getting dirty my fault?

I'll tell you who's a real pain, Sill. It's always "Look at the pretty flowers on the sill." If it weren't for me, all Sill would be holding is a pot full of dirt—no light, no flowers. But I'm a pain right!

Sash understands. He's always lifting me up when I'm down and gently lowers me into position when the air gets uncomfortably cool. Yup, Sash is okay, and nobody ever refers to him as a pain, unless one of his cord's snaps.

What it all comes down to is respect. I get no respect! Guess that's how life is. Those of us that quietly go along doing our jobs, not being flashy or striving for glory, are invisible, which is what I'm supposed to be. What a pain it is being a pane.

Survival Sense

Some places put my internal alarm systems on active standby. *Alma Latinas* was just such a place. Sure, I'd visited this cantina before with several friends, but never alone. Gringos never visit this part of Nuevo Laredo alone, and I know this, so what the hell am I doing here? When you're twenty and bulletproof, in your mind anyway, no place is off-limits.

The evening started with four of us doing a cantina crawl. As the night stretched on, several of the guys met some virtuous senoritas, and I knew I wouldn't be seeing them until sometime tomorrow morning. Robert, of the weak constitution, and my remaining companion, had faded back across the border an hour ago. That left me drifting around places I shouldn't. Finally, after wandering aimlessly for some time, I saw a sign, not from God, but more realistically from the Devil. This sign was multi-colored neon and made a buzzing sound. My salvation, *Alma Latinas*.

When I walked through the door, the interior assaulted all my senses. Loud mariachi music played. Dull yellow lit the interior, so I had to strain my eyes to navigate my way to the bar. The place smelled of stale beer and tequila with just a hint of vomit. As I ran my hand along the bar, I could feel my fingers stick to the surface. My shoes had already become entrapped in the flypaper that was the floor. I ordered a shot of tequila, the good stuff with the worm in the bottom of the bottle, and tried to drink without grimacing.

It didn't take long before a couple of large, well-tattooed gentlemen, wearing leather vests with the word Banditos emblazoned on the back, stood on either side of me. The larger one spoke in a Texas drawl. "What in the hell are you doing in here alone boy?" That's when my "Survival Sense" kicked in.

I knew these guys. We Air Force pukes, as they fondly referred to us, and the Banditos,

Texas's chapter of the Hells Angels, had occasionally partied together. Usually all went well until too much beer flowed. Once we reached that point, it was time to bail in a hurry or see the inside of a Mexican jail. My senses told me that the situation was almost at that tipping point.

I exchanged pleasantries with the gentlemen for a short time hoping the shorter of the two, only six feet three inches, didn't remember our last encounter when I had gifted him a black eye. At an opportune moment, I excused myself and feigned heading for the men's room. No one with working olfactory senses goes in that room. The ruse worked, and I skirted the far wall making it to the exit. As I started walking out the door, I heard a large crash as a table collapsed under the weight of a person who had been thrown onto it.

My departure was none too soon. The local Policia were already exiting their cars, batons in hand.

Off toward the East, I could see the hint of the morning sun peeking over the horizon. Thanks to my "Survival Sense," I had lived to see another tequila sunrise.

The Gift of Time

We left the opulent dining room and retired to a small, well-appointed library. Small is a relative term, as Jack McCabe doesn't own anything small. Why should he? Jack has the dubious distinction of being the world's first trillionaire. No matter how much money a person can amass in a lifetime, it still comes down to how much time you have before your clock runs down to zero.

Jack is rapidly approaching that end. His body is a weak, gnarled shell that has to be transported by a powered chair. He has lost all his hair, and his senses of smell and hearing are fading fast. Jack's eyes, although requiring glasses to see clearly, still show the fierce determination of a world-class predator. Solving the time problem is why McCabe had his men bring me, Michael White, to his estate.

"I must say, Mr. McCabe, I mean Jack, I'm sure that was the best meal ever served to a kidnap victim."

"Come now, Michael, don't you think kidnap is a rather strong word?"

"If two armed men arrived at your door and told you that you were required to accompany them to my house, and no was not an option, what would you call it?" I countered.

Jack chuckled hoarsely. "They would never have made it past the front gate."

"I have no front gate or personal security service, so I guess I'm at a definite disadvantage. All that aside, why have you brought me here?"

"Well, let's start with something simple. Who is Michael White? I've traced you back about thirty years, but then you disappear. There is no digital footprint, no birth or death records, and no old credit reports; nothing that would verify you ever existed. How is that possible?"

Before I could answer, Jack's great-grandson, Peter, came bursting into the room with all the exuberance of a 4-year-old. "Come see what I made for you grandpa!"

Jack was both annoyed and amused by the child's determination and excitement.

"Go with him," I said. "It's not like I'll be going anywhere soon. Besides, time with your family is too precious to waste when there is so little of it left."

Jack gave me a knowing look and replied, "You're right. Please make yourself at home. I'll be back after I've examined this new masterpiece of Peter's."

Jack and Peter left the room, and I poured myself another snifter of brandy. I settled into a comfortable chair and thought about the question... *"Who is Michael White?"*

1349

I was born Michel LeBlanc to a French peasant family in the year of Our Lord 1349. The Black Death was at its peak, claiming over a third of Europe's population. The plague had taken my father a week before I was born and my mother three days after she gave birth. A 12-year-old girl heard me crying as she passed our hut. Wanting to offer assistance, she entered the one-room dwelling and found me lying next to my dead mother. Antoinette, my rescuer, wrapped me in the only clean blanket she could find and took me to a wet nurse. After my hunger was satisfied, I stopped crying and quickly fell asleep. Renée, my nurse, and my mother had been friends. When Antoinette told her how she found me, Renée decided to care for me as long as she could.

After six years of struggling to feed her children plus me, Renée went to the local priest for help. Monsignor Jacque was getting on in years and decided he could use a house boy, so I went to live with him. In return for working in his garden, cleaning the rectory and church, feeding the animals, and a myriad of odd jobs, I received food, clothing, a place to sleep in the hayloft, and most importantly, an education. Only the clergy and noblemen knew how to read and write in the 1300s. With knowledge comes value, and often power; my value to the priest grew as his eyesight dimmed.

Time passed; each year was much like the one before—work, study, and run errands. As I walked back to the rectory early one evening, I came upon a man lying in the gutter. He had been beaten and robbed by highwaymen and left for dead. I helped him to his feet as best a 12-year-old boy could, and somehow got him to my hayloft. I never told the priest I had given shelter to this man.

He healed remarkably fast, and by the evening of the third day, he felt strong enough to continue his journey. I asked him to stay one more night, because it was safer to travel during the day. The man, whose name I never knew, looked into my eyes with an intensity I had never seen anyone exhibit before. It felt like he was peering into my soul, the very essence of my being. I cannot describe the strange sensation that shot through me, and then the uneasiness was gone. It seemed as though the whole thing never happened, and he continued the conversation by agreeing to stay one more night and went back to his mound of straw to sleep.

When I awoke the next morning, the man was gone. By my sleeping pallet was a note that read:

```
My friend,
I   have   looked   into   your   soul   and
found you worthy.
I   have   bestowed  on  you  a  great  gift,
although  at  times  you  may  feel  it  is
a curse.
Use it with great discretion.
All will become clear to you in time.
```

I searched the whole stable for this supposed gift but found nothing. There was much to do, so I tucked the paper in with my meager belongings and started the day's chores. It didn't take long for my adolescent brain to entirely forget about the man, the note, and the supposed gift.

The Present

Jack and Peter returned to the library. Peter, as excited as before, exclaimed, "Look what I drew for Grandpa. He really likes it, do you?"

On the paper, drawn in crayon, was a sketch of the mansion showing Peter's grandfather in his motorized wheelchair, sitting in the entryway, surveying his domain. The drawing was remarkably detailed for a 4-year-old.

"That's a fine drawing, Peter. You have a talent for art," I said as the boy stood there beaming.

"Peter, go and fetch some paper and crayons for Mr. White. He is a real artist; maybe he'll draw us a picture."

"Okay, Grandpa!" Peter ran out of the room in search of supplies.

I stared at Jack and asked, "How do you know about my sketches?"

"In good time, Sir. In good time."

Peter returned promptly and handed me several blank sheets of paper and a box of crayons.

"What would you like me to draw for you, Peter?"

Jack interjected, "How about a picture of what Peter will look like when he is 40 years old?"

"That's an odd request. How am I supposed to know what Peter will look like when he's 40?"

"Not all that odd for a person with your talent, I would think. I hear you can draw amazing likenesses of people, either from their past or their distant future."

"I'm not sure where you received your information, but you must have me confused with someone else."

I turned to Peter. "How about a drawing of a wild horse?"

"Yes, Sir. I like horses a lot." Peter was bursting with youthful enthusiasm.

I began to draw, all the while keeping a wary eye on Jack McCabe.

1362

Etienne de Poissy, the Archbishop of Paris, was returning from Avignon and the election of Pope Urban V. Daylight was running out, and the Archbishop decided to stay the night visiting his old friend, Monsignor Jacque. The two companions spent the evening amiably discussing church matters and learning of each other's recent experiences.

The Archbishop noticed the teenager attending them and inquired about him. Father Jacque couldn't sing my praises enough. He talked about my brilliant mind, aptitude for languages (now fluent in French, Latin and Greek) and my ability to draw lifelike portraits. "I've taught him all I know. What he needs is a first-rate scholar to tutor him."

"If he's that good," replied the Archbishop, "I can arrange to continue his education with the Benedictines, providing he is prepared to move to Paris."

I couldn't believe my ears—move to Paris, the City of Lights. How my life was about to change—from being born in a poor serf's hut to being taught by scholars. I packed my meager belongings, including the letter from the mysterious stranger, and joined the Archbishop's entourage when it left the next morning.

1366

I spent the next four years studying under the Benedictine monks at the Abbey of Saint Germaine-des-Prés, located on the outskirts of Paris. It was a great time to be a young scholar. Even though the Hundred Years War was raging on, King Charles V had regained much of the land lost to the English, and the age of the Renaissance had begun. I learned Italian and Spanish and even a smattering of English. My mathematics were strong and my geography passable.

What set me apart was my sketching ability. Because of my connection to the Archbishop, I spent a lot of time at court. I sketched noblemen, ladies, and occasionally the king. My work was unique from other artists because of my ability to draw not how my subjects looked in the present, but how they had looked in the past. Also, for those adventurous enough to want to see, I could show them how they might look in twenty or more years. My sketches amused many, but some whispered that I might be a practitioner of the dark arts and sorcery.

It seemed that the rumors gained traction the longer I stayed at court. The king died in 1380. I had lived at the palace off and on for fourteen years and appeared to have stopped aging once I reached my eighteenth birthday. I was twenty-seven but looked a good deal younger. The new king was incompetent and, having lost much of the land his father had liberated, looked for someone to blame. A sorcerer would make the perfect scapegoat.

I had earned a considerable amount of money selling my work and, having developed a strong sense of self-preservation, I left Paris and France before things became too dangerous, and I lost my head.

1461

For the next 80 years, I wandered through Europe working as a translator, scribe, and sketch artist. Weary of traveling, I reached The Republic of Genoa and decided to stop for a while. These respites would last for no more than ten to fifteen years. After five years or so, the people I met when I first arrived would begin to glance at me furtively. Questions would arise in a half-joking, half-serious manner as to how I maintained my youth. At first, I could misdirect the inquiries by joking or ignoring the question. As time went by, the questions became more accusatory, and I would be compelled to move on.

Shortly after arriving in Genoa, I came upon merchants selling their wares at the open-air market. Feeling hungry, my eyes were drawn to a cheese vendor a short distance away. A boy of approximately ten years of age tended the stand with his mother. Suddenly, from around the corner came an out of control ox pulling a lumber cart. Everything happened so fast that the boy had no chance to escape the collision. Large wheels of cheese and broken pieces of cart were scattered everywhere and pinned the boy against the nearby building. With the debris removed, it was clear he was severely injured. I was one of the first on the scene and administered aid as best I could.

The injured boy's mother, Susanna, grabbed my arm and pleaded with me to save him. "I will gladly give my life in exchange for that of Christoffa's."

"Are you sure that's what you want?" I asked.

"Yes, I will give anything to save my son."

I knew at this moment that the same mystical gift that was keeping me young could also save the boy if I felt he was worthy. There was a price to pay though. His mother would have to give some of her life. Susanna was young, only 26, and by looking into her life force I could tell she would live until her 65th birthday. Christoffa's life was slowly draining away. If I used some of his mother's life to save his, was he worthy of such a gift? I peered into his young eyes and by doing so, into his future. If he lived, he would become a great explorer and discover a new land.

"Your son will live, but your life will be cut short by eleven years. Is this what you want, Susanna?"

"Yes, yes, anything for my Christoffa!"

It only took a few seconds, and the transfer was complete. The boy's eyes became alert, and I could tell that his internal injuries were already starting to heal. A couple of days later, I revisited the repaired cheese stand where Susanna Colombo and her son were back at work tending to customers. As I approached, the boy immediately ran up to me.

"Thank you for saving me. I will never forget your kindness."

"Don't thank me; thank your mother. It was her gift that saved you. I was just the bridge that allowed the gift to be delivered. When you are older you will achieve great things. People will speak of you with great reverence and remember you throughout the ages. You will be celebrated by the name Christopher Columbus, but you will always know where you came from. Your mother will be very proud of your accomplishments.

1658

It's amazing how much ground can be covered in 200 or so years. I spent 100 years traveling from one Italian city state to another. I met great artists and builders, always being careful not to garner any uncomfortable questions or looks. Escaping people's curiosity had turned into a game for me. Stay for a while, meet new people, and earn enough money to continue my journey. I would help where I could, then leave. By doing some basic math, I worked out that a fifty-year block of time equaled one year of aging for me.

My wanderings finally took me to England. The country was in political unrest. Cromwell and his minions had replaced the monarchy, and neighbor turned on neighbor, suspecting one another of being Royalist. The Black Death had ravaged the large cities and the overall mood was one of despair. Not a welcoming place to visit.

During the autumn of 1658 a massive storm bore into England knocking down trees and buildings, and capsizing ships. I was on the outskirts of the village of Woolesthorpe when it became quite clear that I needed to find shelter from the approaching storm. A farm house with a large barn was close by so I decided to take refuge there. As I approached the structure, I noticed a boy about 15-years of age jumping from a window and marking his landing spot. I watched with interest as the boy repeated the process multiple times.

Curiosity trumped my need for anonymity, so I approached the boy and introduced myself. He was so engrossed in what I thought was a game, that he hardly paid any attention to me.

When I asked him why he was doing the same thing over and over he replied, "I'm trying to measure the effect of the wind on my trajectory."

This was no ordinary teenage farm boy. He told me his name was Isaac and he was sure his mother wouldn't mind if I took shelter in the barn during the tempest.

The storm finally passed and it was time for me to be on my way. First, I walked to the house so I could thank the owner for giving me shelter. Isaac's mother, Hannah, answered the door and I could tell by her expression she had no idea I had stayed in the barn. I told her about my meeting with her son and asked if Isaac was available for me to say good bye. She called for Isaac and he came to the door, immediately apologizing to his mother for forgetting to tell her about me. I reached into my pack and withdrew a sketch of an older man.

I explained to Isaac, "This is you as an adult. The man in this picture will be responsible for unlocking some of the biggest secrets of the universe. The name Isaac Newton will be venerated for centuries as the person who discovered gravity. I wish there was more I could give you, but it's not possible."

I turned and walked away leaving Isaac studying his future self. Several weeks later, I boarded a ship for the New World.

The Present

I completed Peter's sketch of a wild horse running free across the plains. It was actually a memory from the time I had spent with the Cherokee around two hundred years earlier. Of course, Peter didn't know that, he just liked the drawing. He waved it in front of his great grandfather then ran off to show it to the house staff, leaving Jack and I alone once again.

"I guess it's time we cut to the chase," Jack said. "You may not recognize me, but if you use your special ability it will all come back to you. Go ahead, don't just look at me, look into me and you'll know."

Keeping up the pretense of ignorance no longer seemed to be a viable option, so I stared into the other man's soul. His life flashed in my mind like a movie on fast forward. What I saw was, Khaled, Jack's real name, standing in the temple of Ra along with several other acolytes. They were sacrificing a young boy in an attempt to capture his life force. They hoped Ra would grant them, if not immortality, at least an exceptionally long life with the ability to replenish their life force from time to time.

Next, Khaled began traveling from location to location, and from century to century, absorbing some lives and granting extended life to others. The chronicle slowed during 1361 when he was cared for by a 12-year-old boy (me) after being beaten and left for dead. Khaled (Jack) was the stranger who gave me this gift.

A smile stretched across Jack's withered lips. "So young one, you start to understand who I am. I have helped some and hurt some, depending on whether I felt they were worthy or not. You are the only one I gave the full gift to. Now I need your help once again. As you can see, I'm dying. I chose to fall in love and have heirs, which dissolved my contract with Ra. You can give me my youth back."

Jack's request brought back memories of Madeline…

1815

During the battle of New Orleans in 1815 I discovered the limits of my power. I met Denis de Lu Ronde while staying in New Orleans. We became friends, but it was his cousin, Madeline, who I was fascinated with. He invited me to his plantation, and knowing Madeline was going to be there, I eagerly accepted. My elation quickly turned to despair on the first night at Villeré Plantation when the British Expeditionary Force over ran the grounds and mortally wounded Madeline. I tried desperately to save her, but without another's life force it was impossible. Even my extraordinary abilities had limits…

The Present

"I tried restoring someone's life and without a willing donor I wasn't able to," was my reply to Jack. "Even if I could do it, why would I? Besides, viewing our first meeting, I also saw who you have resuscitated. Attila the Hun, Vlad the Impaler, Rasputin, Jack the Ripper, even Hitler, are all people you found worthy. Why would I want to save someone with such poor judgement? I also saw how you became so wealthy. Of course, I'm wealthy too. It's impossible to live this long and not gain wealth. Unlike you, I didn't lie, swindle and sanction murder to become rich. Besides, if I were to grant you this request who would be willing to give you their life force?"

"You've already met him," replied Jack. "Peter has a strong life force, and sacrificing him will please Ra and restore me. You see, I knew I was coming to my end, so I planned for my continuation by having a family. I just needed to find you to complete the process."

Jack then reached behind his back and brought his hand forward holding a semiautomatic pistol. "Now let's go find Peter, shall we?"

I remained seated and smiled at Jack. "Your plan is flawed Jack," I said. "I'm the only one who can change your situation, so you can't shoot me. Nothing you do can make me help you. I've lived a long time and if I die tonight, I can honestly say I've left the world a better place. Can you say the same Jack? Peter will grow into a fine man. He will use his inherited wealth to change the world for the better. Oh, one more thing, when I looked into your life force, I saw that tonight, actually this very hour, is your last on earth. I'm sure you and Ra, or whoever is in charge now, will have a lot to talk about."

Rising from my chair I said to Jack, "I'm going to find Peter now. He'll need guidance in the coming years."

As I walked down the hall, I heard the muffled sound of a gunshot. A small smile crossed my lips as I opened the door to Peter's room; secure in the knowledge that there was no one left alive to threaten his future.

Mark A. Gagnon

Ice and Fire

How can I feel this cold and not be dead? I'm wearing a jacket and gloves, but nothing designed to stave off this type of arctic cold. If I don't start a fire soon, rescuers will find my body encased in a sheath of ice. When I awoke this morning, the highlight of the day was supposed to be observing the Northern Lights, not trying to remain alive.

The sign in the lobby of the Fairbanks Hilton displayed panoramic mountain vistas and a brilliant ribbon of light known as the Aurora Borealis. For $500 the pilot of a single-engine Cessna offered to take his passenger on a twilight flight over the Gates of the Arctic National Park to Prudhoe Bay. During this time of year, the Northern Lights were guaranteed to be spectacular. The next day we would fly back to Fairbanks observing the abundant wildlife from the sky.

It would have been a great trip if not for a flock of migrating Canadian Geese. We were approximately midway into our journey when a loud bang came from the middle of the plane. Two more strikes followed; one to the nose of the aircraft, which damaged the propeller, the second to the windscreen, which shattered and injured the pilot. The engine sputtered and stalled, and our only option was whether our descent would be controlled or nose-in. The pilot extended the flaps and lined up for a landing on a downward sloping snowfield above the treeline.

As we plummeted to the ground, I gathered a few nearby items placing them in a canvas bag positioned between the seats. The Cessna made a loud scraping noise as it transitioned from air to ground, then it began to slide like a snowboard. We were picking up speed as the aircraft approached the end of the ice field and the edge of a 200 feet precipice. I looked to the pilot for ideas and realized he hadn't survived the crash; a wing strut was protruding from his chest. There was only one thing left to do. I grabbed the canvas bag and jumped from the fuselage, hoping I would clear the tail section. My body horseshoed around a nearby boulder as the aft section of the plane passed by and careened over the edge of the cliff.

It wasn't long before the horror of what I had just witnessed, and the feeling of sheer relief that I survived, was replaced by the reality of biting cold, and the remoteness of my location. For any chance of survival, I needed to descend below the timberline. A quick search recovered my bag that contained a flashlight, hatchet, cabling used to tie down the plane, and a small first aid kit. My pants and jacket pockets contained some paper money, a few coins, and a package of individually wrapped sticks of chewing gum. It wasn't much, but it was all I had.

Fortunately, between the moon and the Northern Lights, the flashlight was unnecessary for this leg of the trip. At this altitude, the snow glistened, reflecting enough light that I could make my way down the mountainside without stumbling. Once I reached the trees, the flashlight would be necessary, unless I could start a fire.

It took about an hour of steady walking before I passed small shrubs and some stunted pine trees. I should soon find enough fuel to start a fire, provided my ignition method worked. The further into the forest I went, the more the sounds around me changed. Above the treeline, the only sounds were the moaning of the wind and the snow crunching under my boots. The wind remained, augmented by the rustling of branches, the scurrying of small animals, and one other thing, the howling of wolves.

I reached a clearing and decided it was time to put my firemaking skills to the test. I started by gathering some dried leaves and dead twigs, which I arranged teepee style against each other. I then took a piece of cotton gauze from the first aid kit and wove it between the sticks. Now for the moment of truth, because I was slowly freezing to death and I could hear the wolves cautiously creeping closer. I unscrewed the flashlight and removed one of the batteries, then unwrapped a stick of gum. I carefully tore the middle out of the aluminum-backed paper, so only a thread remained to connect the two halves. I only had one shot at this working. The wolves were knocking at the proverbial door. By holding the untorn part of the wrapper on either end of the battery, current flowed through the aluminum setting the paper on fire, which in turn ignited the gauze, then the leaves and twigs. I added larger pieces of wood until I had a very comfortable campfire blazing away. Like most wild animals, the wolves were frightened of fire and remained in the shadows; eventually wandering off in search of easier prey.

It took the rescue team three days to spot the smoke from my fire. During the time I was stranded above the Arctic Circle, I was fortunate to witness the most beautiful night skies I will ever see.

Mark A. Gagnon

Glimpse into the Future

I love my life! I rise each morning before Alice and the kids, work out for about an hour in the basement gym, and then wake them up to start their day. While I'm showering, Alice is making breakfast while encouraging Billy and Jane to move faster so they won't miss the bus. It's a "Leave It to Beaver" kind of life. My job will never make me rich, but it is fulfilling and an easy commute as well. Yes, I love my life and everything about it except for one thing, the incessant and ever-present background noise.

It started as a faint white noise that could be easily ignored. As the days passed the noise increased in volume, and I was able to make out distinct sounds: the soft beep-beep of a machine, rubber-soled shoes on a tiled floor, vague sounds that resembled distant conversations. All this occurred in my subconscious while my life happened around me. There were soccer and little league games to attend, parent-teacher conferences, and those special times when the kids were visiting friends, and Alice and I were alone.

It was during one of these special nights when, out of nowhere, Alice said, "I know you'll be leaving soon, but I wish it weren't so." What in the world was she talking about? Then the background noise intensified to the point that I could no longer ignore it.

What I originally interpreted as white noise evolved into a heated discussion between a man and a woman. The woman, in the most irritating voice I had ever heard, was complaining that there had been no improvement in over ten months and the maintenance was a drain on her bank account. She wanted them to "pull the plug and be done with it." The man, with great restraint, told her that there had been signs of improvement and it would be a grave mistake to curtail treatment.

Finally, I'd had enough and bellowed in a scratchy voice, "Will you tone it down and take it outside, I have a headache."

There was a flurry of activity as medical staff rushed into the room and attended to me. The irritating woman was my actual wife, Claudia. She slinked away while no one was paying attention. The next day a doctor and another man sat with me. The doctor said I had taken a headfirst fall down a flight of stairs at my house, cracked my skull, and became comatose.

"What stairs?" I asked. "My house is a single story. The cracked skull was the result of Claudia hitting me with a heavy candlestick. We were arguing about her plans for a trip to Cabo that we couldn't afford. As I walked away, she screamed that I was worth more dead than alive and hit me in the head."

The other man stood, identified himself as a police detective, and left the room. My house was his next stop.

About a week later, the hospital discharged me. All Claudia said to me during a brief conversation over a prison phone was, "You've never done anything well. You couldn't even die right!"

My life eventually returned to normal. One day while waiting in line at a fast-food restaurant, I noticed a woman who looked vaguely familiar. We reached the counter at the same time to pick up our food and realized that our orders had been switched. We smiled at each other as we exchanged items and introduced ourselves. Her name was Alice.

One Man's Trash...

Jake returned from his tour in Vietnam on January 31, 1969, and proceeded directly into the arms of his high school sweetheart, Jackie. Several months later, they were married and began building their life together. Like most newlyweds, they were long on needs and short on cash, so every Saturday they visited the local thrift shops searching for items to furnish their new home. It was on one such excursion to a Salvation Army store that Jackie's keen eye spotted a plate, cup, and saucer that she had to have.

The set was made of fine bone china and edged in what appeared to be gold leaf. A picture of what could only be the White House was displayed in the center of the plate. The cup and saucer carried the embossed eagle symbol of the United States. When Jackie turned each piece over, she saw the numbers 1811 followed by the initials DM, which she thought was probably the manufacturer's mark. These items would be the perfect centerpiece to display in the hutch Jake had just finished restoring. Jake could never say no to Jackie when she wanted something, so they left the shop with the china.

It has been said that time is a thief, and for the happy couple this was especially true. One minute they were newlyweds and the next they were confronting retirement. Faced with a drastic reduction in income they reluctantly realized that downsizing was the only way they could survive the so-called "golden years." The couple decided to start with an auction, and what didn't sell would be placed in a yard sale. After the yard sale the remaining items would go to the Salvation Army to help some young couple.

Jake remained in touch with an old army buddy who was in the antique appraisal and auction business, so he asked for his help. Most of the items Jake and Jackie had accumulated over their life together had a lot of sentimental value but not a lot of cash value. Jake's friend wandered through the house, placing approximate prices on the items for auction. He stopped directly in front of the plate, cup, and saucer. He gingerly inspected each item with great care, set the last piece down and asked, "Do you know what you have here?"

Puzzled, both replied "No."

Jake blurted out, "Just an old place setting, right?

"Well, you're half right, it is old. In 1811 Dolly Madison commissioned a new set of china to replace the chipped and cracked White House china. It was put into service three days before the start of the War of 1812. When the British and Canadian forces conquered DC they occupied the White House just long enough to enjoy a meal on this very china. After the supper was over, they set fire to the house and all its contents. The First Lady organized a crew to salvage as many valuable items as was possible, including the portrait of George Washington. The dishes were left behind. Until today only five pieces were known to exist, now there are eight. At auction these should bring at least $500,000."

At first the old couple were speechless, then Jackie began to sob knowing that their future was finally secure. Jake, sporting a huge grin said, "I guess the old saying is true. One man's trash is another man's treasure."

Happy Birthday Mikey

Chance brought the three together; friendship formed a spiritual bond that would last throughout their lives. Dan, the son of a Boston factory worker; Mikey, from a family of Louisiana Cajun shrimpers; and Luis, a first-generation American from California, met at the Army's AIT (Advanced Infantry Training) school. Even though they hailed from different parts of the country, the trio shared many similarities including the same birthday. The primary reason the three enlisted was to create a better life for themselves and their families. If the road to accomplishing that goal wound its way through the jungles of Vietnam, then so be it.

They'd been in country for seven months and seen more than their fair share of action, but remained unscathed. Today's mission, a simple enemy troop recon, didn't appear to be anything out of the ordinary. Besides, it was their shared birthday, so what could go wrong? In honor of their special day the Three Musketeers, as they were now known, would stay toward the back of the platoon babysitting a reporter embedded with the company.

All went as expected for the first hour of the mission, then hell's gates flew open spewing fire, lead, and all manner of destruction. The front of the unit suffered the most damage, allowing enough time for the trio and the reporter to dive for cover in different directions. Before they had time to fully assess their situation, a dull thud came from the ground next to Mikey. "Grenade," he yelled, and in one self-sacrificing movement threw himself on top of the bomb.

As the dust and debris settled, Dan was able to see what remained of Mikey. Luis was also injured, missing a right foot and suffering from shock. What Dan did next, remains somewhat fuzzy even to this day. He remembers picking up a 30-caliber machine gun and walking forward. As one gun would run out of ammunition, he'd pick up another weapon from a dead comrade or fallen foe; it didn't matter. When his walk finished, 45 Vietnamese Regulars lay dead around him. He returned to Luis and found the reporter had already applied a tourniquet on his right leg. Dan used branches fastened together with shoelaces from fallen soldier's boots to construct a litter, then placed his friends on it. With the help of the reporter, Dan dragged his comrades out of the jungle. It was only after they were back at base camp that Dan realized he'd been shot three times.

Dan and Luis, along with Mikey's flag-draped coffin, returned to the U.S. on the same aircraft. A plethora of medals and citations followed. When Dan was well enough, he was released from the hospital and honorably discharged. Luis would never leave the hospital as his mental condition deteriorated to near catatonic. Dan continued to visit him once a week.

Today was the trio's 69th birthday and 50 years since that fateful day in Nam. Dan had scraped by on his disability pension and whatever menial jobs he could find. Lack of sleep had taken its toll. Falling asleep was not the problem; it was the reoccurring nightmare his brain generated each night. The battle was on constant replay, and he had no off button.

Dan got up, folded his bed back into the couch and decided to have a birthday party. He dressed in his best clothes, and on his way to visit Luis made two stops—one to the party store and one to the bakery. Dan entered the V.A. long-term care facility with a large bag in one hand and a cake box in the other and proceeded directly to Luis's ward.

He walked past the duty nurse, a humorless woman in her 50s. By the time she unfolded herself from behind her desk, Dan was already in Luis's room and had blocked the door with a chair wedged under the doorknob. Dan began distributing party hats and favors. When security finally arrived, Dan was narrating the saga of the Three Musketeers from Vietnam. The guards, mostly ex-military, recognized that this wasn't some random act, but a celebration of a fallen comrade's life and sacrifice. Two of the guards escorted the nurse back to her station and politely but firmly told her to stay out of it.

The party lasted less than an hour, and after Dan cleaned up, he said to Luis, "I hope you enjoyed our birthday party."

Luis reached up taking Dan by the shoulders and replied, "Mikey and I thought it was great!" Then he slumped back into his million-mile stare.

Dan opened the ward door and stepped into the hallway fully expecting to be arrested. Instead, the guards lined both sides of the corridor, snapped to attention, and gave him a crisp salute. The nurse scowled but said nothing. Dan walked across the parking lot to his 1996 Toyota Corolla and drove back to his one-room studio apartment. He was exhausted from the day's events and couldn't wait to fall asleep. Somehow, he knew that he had found that off button to the nightmare, and at least for tonight, he would enjoy undisturbed, blissful sleep.

Happy Birthday, Mikey!

Mark A. Gagnon

Under Pressure

The *USS Hawaii*, a fast-attack nuclear submarine, finished replenishing supplies at the naval base in Yokosuka, Japan. Once underway, they would prowl the Pacific in search of threats to the US and its allies for the next three months. All 15 officers and 113 enlisted personnel reported for duty; the order was given to cast off, and the ship was soon underway.

During the whole departure procedure, it was hard for Ensign Mike Monahan to control his enthusiasm. He had graduated from the U.S. Naval Academy just two months earlier, and this was his first duty assignment.

Relief was the best way to describe how Chief of Boat, Master Chief Jack Smith, felt. The old salt had 28 years of sea duty under his belt and was well aware of all the stupid screw-ups that can happen while transitioning from harborside to the open sea. This crew had their act together, he admitted to himself. Jack had sailed under Captain Wallace and several other officers under his command, so he knew what was expected of him and the other enlisted men. Yes, everything seemed shipshape.

It took less than a week for the Ensign and the Chief to have their first confrontation. Life aboard a sub is less formal than on a surface ship. That's not to say all military bearing is dispensed with, but when more than 100 people live in close quarters, small infractions are often overlooked. Ensign Monahan hadn't been taught that at the Naval Academy and regularly reprimanded the crew for insignificant breaches of protocol. Finally, the Chief felt it was time to intervene.

"Ensign Monahan, a word please," said Chief Smith.

"Yes, Chief, how may I help you?"

"Should you have an issue with any of the crew that doesn't involve a safety situation, would you please bring it to my attention before speaking to the crewmember. As Chief of Boat, it's my job to reprimand as necessary. The other officers, including the Captain, adhere to this policy. I know these men, and can point out problems to them without lowering morale."

"At the Academy, we were taught that a good officer fixes small problems on the spot before they become large problems. Unless the Captain orders me to do things differently, that's what I will continue to do."

Before Jack could reply, a seaman from the galley interrupted them. "Excuse me for interrupting, Sir, Chief, but you need to come to the Captain's wardroom, right now," blurted out the panic-stricken sailor.

Captain Wallace and all his officers were in a meeting, with the exception of Monahan who was the designated on-duty officer. When the three men arrived at the wardroom, two crewmembers stopped them. Through the porthole of the closed door, Chief Smith and Ensign Monahan saw fourteen dead officers and one dead cook. Monahan had never seen a dead person before and traumatized, he recoiled from the horrific scene. This wasn't the Chief's first dead body. He was able to stay focused on the task at hand.

"Do you know how this happened?" the Chief asked..

The seaman, who was assistant cook, spoke up. "Cook took a carton of eggs from the provisions locker. He went to use one of the eggs but stopped when he noticed something wasn't right. It looked like there was a tiny needle hole sealed with glue. He checked the remaining eggs and found they had all been tampered with. Cook was concerned and decided to immediately bring the suspect eggs to the Captain's attention. I was standing in the doorway as the officers took turns inspecting the eggs, then one them dropped an egg by mistake. Immediately they all began choking and gasping for air. I closed the door and came to find you."

"Ensign Monahan, what do you make of this?" asked Chief Smith.

"How the hell do I know! We need to surface and air the ship out! Call for help and get some instructions from headquarters! My God, what a mess!"

"Ensign, walk with me. As the highest-ranking officer, you are now the acting Captain. The men are looking to you for cool-headed, rational thinking and a calm demeanor. If you aren't up to the task, I'll have to ask you to retire to your quarters until you can pull yourself together. I'm also available for advice should you need it. Are we clear?"

"Crystal," replied the Ensign as he straightened his posture and calmed his nerves. "What would you suggest we do next Chief?"

"I would suggest we deploy our low-frequency antenna to communicate with HQ but remain submerged. Using sonar, we can tell what's around us, but we have no clue what's waiting for us in the air. This is probably a random act of terror, but we can't be sure. Once we contact command, they can give us further instructions. What are your orders, Sir?"

"I believe I'll follow your suggestions, Chief. Please let me know when contact has been established with HQ. And Chief, thanks." Chief Smith gave the acting Captain a crisp salute and carried out his orders.

The *Hawaii* returned to port two days later. NCIS determined the pathogen was Sarin gas injected into the egg shells after the contents had been drained. No group claimed responsibility for the attack, probably because the sub made it back to port. Chief Smith received a commendation for valor by the recently promoted Lieutenant J.G. Monahan.

Once things returned to normal, Chief Smith decided it was time to retire. The new Lieutenant remained in the navy, eventually retiring as a Captain. He remained forever grateful to Master Chief Smith for his guidance on that fateful day.

Tick...Tick...Tick

Okay, I did volunteer for this job, so I have nothing to complain about. In fairness though, I volunteered shortly after basic while I was in the middle of AIT (Advanced Infantry Training). Running around Afghanistan with a rifle really wasn't my idea of a good time. When a couple of senior sergeants came into our training area asking for a few volunteers for special training, my hand shot up before I even knew what the job was. That's how I ended up in the Army's Bomb Disposal Unit.

Generally, the job has been pretty cool. Most of the time is spent learning about explosive devices and how to disarm them. When we're out in the field, we wear these Michelin Man suits and stop things from going BOOM. As it turns out, I'm good at the job, which is probably why I got called for this one.

I'm currently lying on my side, in a tunnel under the main hangar at Bagram Air Force Base. It must have taken months to dig, and it was only found by accident a couple of hours ago. The call went out to get the bomb squad on sight ASAP. That was over an hour and a half ago, but we only arrived fifteen minutes ago. You've got to love interbranch communication. The bomb is here because the President was supposed to land in approximately ten minutes. Now he's flying in circles waiting for the all clear and I'm in this cramped hole with a bomb the size of a VW Bug.

Tick... Tick... Tick...

Most IEDs are fairly simple. There's a power source, a triggering mechanism, a detonator, and the explosives. This device is much more complicated with wires leading around and through what looks like a backup trigger in case the first one fails. Someone put a lot of thought into designing this, and I now have only three minutes left to disarm it.

Tick... Tick... Tick...

I know from experience that certain wires are dead ends. I focus on a pair of white and black wires in the very back of the bomb that look like they control everything. When I reach around with my pair of wire cutters, my arm moves the control module. Nothing goes boom. That's a very good thing. Under the control panel I see another pair of wires, red and green.

Tick... Tick... Tick...

Now I understand. The black and white wires are decoys. Cut one of them, and everything goes up in a big ball of fire. I need to cut the red or green wire but which one? In times like this, we're taught to go with our gut, but all my gut is saying is that I'd really like a cheeseburger. Red means stop, green means go. Go with your head and cut the red. No time for further deliberation.

Tick... Three... Two...One... Snip!

Mark A. Gagnon

Damn Liberals

"Gentlemen, let me start with introductions," came a voice from a speaker placed in the center of the table. "At the far side of the table is Ramses II, Pharaoh of Egypt during the exodus. To his right Pope Leo X, head of the Roman Catholic Church during the time of Martin Luther and the Great Reformation. Next to him is King George III, England's monarch when the American Revolution occurred. Our next guest is King Louis XVI, the last monarch of France (holding his severed head). Moving on we have Jefferson Davis, president of the Confederate States of America, Adolph Hitler and last but not least, Joseph Stalin. The one thing that you attendees have in common is a distinct hatred of liberals, am I correct?"

All attendees in unison exclaimed, *"Damn Liberals!"*

"I thought as much," said the disembodied voice. "Would anyone care to share?"

"I'll start," Ramses grumbled. "All was going well. Monuments, palaces, pyramids were being built on time and under budget thanks to free slave labor. Then along comes Moses preaching freedom and a Promised Land, and poof, its Exodus time. There went my construction projects!"

Resentfully, the group grumbled, *"Damn Liberals!"*

Pope Leo was next. "My church was the real power during the Dark and Middle Ages. We had Western Europe under our thumb. Sure, there were some Jews, but they were manageable, and the Muslims mainly stayed in the Middle East. All was as it should be until Martin Luther started his Reformation movement. It spread like wildfire, and before it could be stopped, splinter groups were springing up almost every day.

With increasing enthusiasm, *"Damn Liberals!"*

"I had the most powerful navy in the world," lamented George. "North America was our colony and had only the rights we allowed them to have. Revolt over taxes and a lack of representation, preposterous! That's what I thought anyway, then people like Thomas Payne and Sam and John Adams began stirring up the rabble, and they ruined everything."

With gusto, *"Damn Liberals!"*

Louis had nothing to say (because he couldn't). Instead, he placed his severed head on the table before him and pounded his fists.

Everyone said it for him, *"Damn Liberals!"*

The next person to speak was Jefferson Davis. "We in the South had a wonderful way of life, gentile and refined. It was those crass Northerners with their factories, mechanized harvesting methods, and free-thinking that destroyed our lifestyle. They swooped in, freed our slaves, and carved up our plantations all in the name of human rights and progress."

Bitterly, *"Damn Liberals!"*

By this time, Adolf was red in the face and ready to tell his tale of woe. "My plan was to restore the German people to their rightful place as world dominators. If only I had invaded England instead of only using rockets and bombs, the liberal Americans would have had no place to stage their troops.

Stirred to a near frenzy, "*Damn Liberals!*"

"I had everything working the right way," said Joseph Stalin. "Russians were forced to contribute to the state or be sent to the gulags. We were all of one mind, or else! So, what happens, I die, and not one successor is strong enough to take my place. They let the liberals chip away at what I built until the wall came tumbling down."

Vengeance in their eyes and hatred in their hearts, "*Damn Liberals!*"

The room fell silent. From the far end came a faint click followed by a sliding sound. A well-disguised door slid open, and an impeccably dressed man stepped forward. His skin had a reddish hue, and odd-shaped bumps appeared on either side of his forehead. It became clear as he spoke that he was the moderator heard on the speaker. "Gentlemen, I feel your pain as I too have been fighting this wave of liberalism for eons. I considered myself a liberal in the beginning, trying to change the hierarchy of heaven, but failed. Over the years, one indisputable fact has stood out above all else, when the liberals prevail and achieve their lofty goals, they become conservatives. That's right. The most ardent of liberals will defend his beliefs to the death rather than accept change, making them conservatives."

So, all together now, *"Welcome Liberals, the future of the conservative movement!"*

Mark A. Gagnon

Stan's Reality — Altered

Stan, a 55-year-old traveling salesman, was a Bostonian through and through. The Red Sox, Patriots, Celtics, and Bruins were the only teams worth rooting for. In Stan's world, change can never be a good thing. His third-floor walkup apartment was the same one he and a fellow student rented while attending Suffolk University 35 years ago. The roommate moved on; Stan never did. Why leave a place that felt as comfortable as an old pair of jeans?

Stan thought the same about his job. He originally got the job because his father was one of the company principals. After his father retired, Stan figured out how to keep his job without protection from above. Early in his career, Stan noticed the top producers from the previous year would either have their quotas doubled or their territories reduced. Once this happened, the heavy hitters would move on; the bottom salesmen usually got fired. Stan decided to control his fate by staying right in the middle, making one or two big sales a year to keep the bosses happy, but nothing to put him on top.

Stan's love-life mirrored the rest of his existence. He had several somewhat serious relationships, but when it comes to making a commitment, well, it just isn't him. Why commit to something or someone that could potentially disrupt his life. Besides, there were plenty of ladies out there willing to spend the night for a nice meal, a few drinks, or if things got desperate, cash. The problem at 55, the ladies in the dating pool looked more and more like his retired mother and less and less like the coeds and young career women he used to date. Of course, if he were to take an honest look in the mirror… well no need to go there. Maybe a change in the relationship department was due, just not too much of a change.

Part of Stan's daily routine was to skim through a copy of USA Today. He did this not because he was particularly interested in current events, but because he needed something to talk about to his customers besides Boston sports. One story did catch his attention. Several weeks in a row there were articles about missing middle-aged, single men. The authorities seemed to think it was the work of a serial killer. No bodies were recovered, only the victim's personal effects left in hotel rooms around the country. It was hard to come up with a suspect when there was no body or crime scene.

Interesting, thought Stan, *wonder where the bodies went?*

The second Monday of the month meant it was time for Stan to board an early morning flight from Logan Airport to New Orleans. Stan liked the Big Easy. The city was old, like his Boston, with a vibe of perpetual partying mixed with magic. Most times, it was also a place where an older gentleman could find a younger lady to keep him company for the evening without needing cash.

Stan settled into his window seat, hoping the middle seat would stay empty, when he saw her.

The woman was in her late thirties/early forties, with jet black shoulder-length hair, Middle Eastern complexion and penetrating golden eyes. She was by far the most stunning woman he'd ever laid eyes on, and she sat next to him. His first reaction—sink deeper into his seat and try to disappear. She was so far out of his league, what could he possibly find to say to her.

She looked at Stan and smiled. "It looks like the Pats might make it to the Super Bowl again this year." Stan was flabbergasted! Not only beautiful but a Boston sports fan.

The plane took off, and so did their conversation, covering everything from sports to favorite authors to French Quarter cuisine. Stan asked her name, and she replied, "Lilith."

Jokingly he said, "Like in the TV show Cheers."

She chuckled. "Yes, one of many with my name."

"Wasn't that the name of Adam's first wife before Eve came along?" Stan asked.

Anger flashed in those gold eyes. Stan thought he heard her mumble, "The Bitch," but then the moment was gone as quickly as it had arrived. She smiled again and told Stan not many people knew about that Lilith.

Stan said that he had read a brief passage about the original Lilith but didn't know much about her.

The conversation quickly moved to other things and continued while deplaning. They realized their hotels were on the same block and shared a cab. Lilith's hotel was first, so Stan thought, *It's now or never*, and asked "Would you like to join me for dinner?"

"Yes," she answered. Could this be the woman who would change his life forever?

They agreed to meet at 8:00 p.m. in the lobby of her hotel. Dinner became a blur of wine, food, and laughter. It was over much too soon.

Stan was sure of the answer but asked anyway, "Would you like to come back to my room?"

"My hotel is closer." She had a faraway look in those golden eyes.

They made it back to her room in world record time, the passion built as they fumbled to unlock the door. Once inside, clothes went flying, and the next thing Stan knew, he was on his back in her bed. Something wasn't right. It was that damn ceiling light shining in his eyes. He didn't want to move, but the light switch was on the other side of the room.

Lilith, as though reading his mind, said, "Don't worry about the light, I'll get it." She reached out her arm toward the switch on the opposite wall.

Terror shot through every cell in Stan's body as Lilith's arm stretched across the room. He suddenly remembered the stories of the missing men. Stan tried to push her off him and run, but his body felt encased in quicksand. As her finger reached the light switch, Stan realized he was about to learn the fate of those missing men.

The light and Stan's world went dark.

Mirror Image

Romulus (named after one of the mythical founders of Rome) went about his normal morning routine still half asleep. He had a restless night but didn't remember anything out of the ordinary that kept him awake. Rom shrugged it off, finished his breakfast, and headed for the door. Stepping over the threshold, Rom almost tripped over a small package lying on the porch. He scooped it up and tore it open on the way to the car. The mystery box contained a pocket-size notepad and a metal refillable pen. He took the package, tossed it on the passenger seat, and headed for work.

As he approached a particularly dangerous intersection, two cars collided directly in front of him. Rom was the only witness, and being a responsible citizen remained at the accident scene until the police arrived. Accurate witness statements are always important at accident scenes, so Rom reached in his pocket for his phone to dictate notes. The phone was nowhere to be found. He must have inadvertently left it at the house. Remembering the note pad and pen, Rom snatched them from the passenger seat and began jotting down notes. The police were grateful for his attention to detail.

Rom arrived at work the following day to find a package waiting for him on his desk. None of his co-workers saw it being delivered. He opened it tentatively and discovered a roll of duct tape. "This stuff fixes everything," he mumbled to himself, "but what needs fixing around here?"

A new carpet had been ordered for the office but wouldn't arrive for several more weeks. One well-worn section had developed a tear, and people, especially ladies in heels, were always tripping on it. Rom put the tape to good use covering the damage and garnered the thanks of his fellow workers. At the end of the day he placed the roll of tape in a plastic crate he kept in the trunk. There's no such thing as having too much duct tape.

Day three started in a panic. The alarm failed to go off, and Rom had only minutes to dress and leave for work. A third package greeted him on the porch. "I don't have time for this!" muttered Rom as he scooped up the box and raced to his car. He had almost made it when the latch on his briefcase broke, spilling the contents on the ground. Rom gathered the items and stuffed everything back into the case. He thought about the tape in the trunk but, as he was already late, decided to open the package first. Inside the padded envelope was a wide rubber band perfect for holding the case together.

The fourth day's item was hanging from the knob on his front door. A tire iron was dangling from a length of twine. "This is handy." Thought Rom "I don't own one of these."

As he drove toward the end of his street, he saw a neighbor standing by her somewhat lopsided car. The right rear tire was as flat as the road surface. Rom pulled in behind her and, using his new wrench, had the tire changed in less than fifteen minutes.

Romulus to the rescue! he thought. *I like the sound of that.*

Day five was typical until a FedEx truck pulled up to Rom's house early in the evening and delivered a special-order package. Rom thanked the driver and brought the bundle into the kitchen to open it. He was pleasantly surprised when the content was a filleting knife. He had been invited to a B-B-Q the next day and, fancying himself somewhat of a chef, had volunteered to do the cooking. He knew he hadn't ordered the knife, but he would make good use of it.

Headed for the cookout on day six, Rom heard a terrible screeching and tearing of metal. He could feel the ground shudder even while sitting in his car. Approximately half a mile ahead was a railroad crossing with a derailed Amtrak train lying on its side. Rom arrived before the first responders and, since he'd been trained by the Air Force as a medic, rushed to lend assistance. Rom found the first victim pinned under a piece of wreckage. Being a proactive person, he had grabbed the crate which contained all the items he had received along with other tools. Using his newly acquired tire iron, Rom levered the debris off the victim.

After a quick field exam, he determined the man was suffering from a tension pneumothorax and was suffocating. Rom grabbed the fillet knife and carefully made an incision at the fifth intercostal space. He then disassembled the pen and pushed the pen's barrel into the opening, releasing a gush of air and fluid. Rom secured the pen in place with duct tape. He then used his large rubber band to hold a makeshift splint in place on the man's broken arm.

The emergency responders arrived. They inspected Rom's work and proclaimed his fast action had saved the man's life. Rom was too drained to continue to the cookout and went home.

At home, he headed to the kitchen for a glass of water. Sitting on the counter was a new bottle of Makers Mark bourbon with a note attached.

Drink up hero; you deserve it!

Both fear and anger coursed through his body. *Time to get to the bottom of this!*

He'd installed a new Ring security system and settled in to watch the surveillance video. A man appeared in several segments who looked identical to Rom, but different in some undefinable way. Comprehension hit him like a heavyweight's right cross.

Rom had served in combat and suffered severe head trauma. Besides the physical wounds, the doctors diagnosed him with Dissociative Identity Disorder, aka split personality. As in mythology, Remus was his evil twin. After intensive therapy and some medication, Rom thought he'd locked Remus deep in a dungeon located far in the recesses of his mind. Somehow Remus had escaped. It was Remus who had removed the stop signs at the intersection where the accident occurred, sabotaged his neighbor's tire, and enlarged the tear in the office carpet. It was also Remus who, using Rom's skill as a coder, hacked into Amtrak's system and caused the derailment.

All this was done to satisfy Remus's need to be a hero.

Remus is back in the world, and the age-old battle of Romulus and Remus has resumed.

Mark A. Gagnon

Cryptogram

I started my day as usual: wake up at 6:30, dress in running gear, leave the house by 6:50, try to run a 2-mile course through the park in under 15 minutes. All was going according to plan until halfway through my run when I heard a scraping sound every time I put my right foot down. "So, this is how my day is going to go!" I said to no one in particular and sat on a nearby bench to examine my shoe.

Stuck to the sole was an intricately folded piece of paper held together along the outside edge with glue. Ordinarily, I would have tossed it into the nearby trash bin, but the way it was so carefully folded and sealed piqued my curiosity. I peeled the edge free and unfolded a small page of text.

```
By   opening   this   letter,   you   have
embarked   on   a   journey   that   could
potentially   change   your   life.   Just
```

> solve the cryptogram below and your future is financially secure.
>
> **I want to win it all!**
>
> There is one stipulation. Half of what you win must be given to one or more charities of your choice. Act before the end of today, or your opportunity will be lost.

My curiosity aroused, I put the note in my pocket for later contemplation and finished my run. I proceeded with my routine, rereading the message in between sips of my protein shake. I like puzzles, and this could be a challenge. Time was running short, so the note went into my coat pocket and stayed there until lunchtime.

After reading the message for the third time, I took out a blank sheet of paper and started writing down letter combinations that would reveal a phrase, password, anything that would give me a clue. My co-workers began returning from lunch, and the main topic of conversation was the $400 million Megaball lottery drawing that night. Lottery numbers, could that be the key?

By Combining the letters in each word of the sentence, I acquired their numeric value: I = 9 (ninth letter in the alphabet); want = 58; to = 35; win = 46; it = 29; and all = 25. This is just too strange for me to think it wouldn't work. An eternity passed in the four hours before quitting time, but when five o'clock finally arrived, I was out the door and headed for the closest convenience store to purchase my lottery ticket. I only bought one ticket because I was either right about the code or I wasn't, no hedging my bet. With the ticket safely tucked away in my pants pocket, I went home to await the results.

The evening dragged on endlessly. Finally, the time of reckoning had arrived. The machine was turned on, the balls danced in the air and one by one rolled down the chute. 58, 46, 35, 29, 9, and the mega-ball 25. Joy, bewilderment, terror, pick an emotion and I experienced it. After a sleepless night, I contacted my lawyer and financial advisor, followed by a visit to the lottery commission to claim my prize. It took about a week, but I was the country's newest multimillionaire with a bank account that exceeded $284 million. A deal is a deal, so I wrote a check for $142 million to the Make A Wish Foundation, fulfilling my part of the bargain.

Later that same year I was aboard a private jet heading to Monte Carlo. Next to my drink sat a folded and glued sheet of paper. Nervously, I unsealed it and read the message.

> I'm pleased you were able to decipher the code and claim your prize. Even more importantly, you are a man of integrity and donated as instructed. Life would have been very different had you not followed the directions. Sometime in the future, you will receive instructions on how to pay your good fortune forward. Until then, enjoy your life.

The Good Deed

Well after midnight, with snow swirling across the airport, my flight was the last to arrive. Only five passengers, including me, were left in this wannabe airport by the time my suitcase, sporting a freshly damaged wheel, finally arrived. Adding insult to injury, the shuttle service had stopped running for the night. I now had to schlep my bag with the broken wheel through the heavy, wet snow to the rental car center on the opposite side of the parking lot. At real airports, shuttles ran until the last flight arrived, but not here in Boondock Regional.

Pushing my case in front of me like a makeshift snow plow, I eventually made it to the rental center, pushed through the unshoveled snowdrift that partially covered the entryway, and stumbled inside. The two employees behind the counter looked away from the TV they were watching, gave me an absent-minded head nod, and returned their attention to the screen.

I was cold, wet, tired, and in need of a toilet, so I slogged across the reception area, feet squishing in my sodden shoes, to the men's room. Once situated in a stall, I changed into dry clothes and shoes and headed back to the counter.

The attendants were nowhere to be found, the TV was off, and the lights dimmed. I walked behind the counter and through a doorway leading to a makeshift office/breakroom, also deserted. "So, what else can go wrong?" I said to the empty building. The answer came two minutes after I asked the question.

Returning to the abandoned counter, I rifled through various drawers looking for keys, an emergency number, or anything that could help me contact someone. Something metal towards the back of a floor level cubbyhole caught my eye, so I reached in to retrieve it. A loud snap was followed by my equally loud cry of pain. I withdrew my hand along with a mousetrap attached to two of my fingers.

Okay, enough is enough, and this day needed to be over now! After freeing my damaged fingers from the trap, I walked back to the breakroom where I bought a couple of snacks from the vending machines. Snacks eaten, I shuffled back to a well-worn couch in the waiting area. It didn't take me long to fall into a deep sleep.

A couple of hours later, I was gently nudged to a semi-conscious state by a female who appeared to be in her early twenties. She must have just come in from outside where the blizzard was still raging because there was a faint white glow surrounding her. Still half asleep, I thought the snow caused the effect on her coat refracting the light from the building's inadequate nightlights.

"Sorry to disturb you sir, but I think you would be more comfortable on a cot we have set up in the storage room. The room is much more secure as well, so you won't need to worry about anyone walking off with your belongings."

I happily took her suggestion and followed her to the cot. She moved quietly, as though her feet never touched the ground. When we reached the storage room, I asked her how she managed to get to the building with the storm raging outside.

She offered the hint of a smile and said, "It seems as though I never leave this place," then turned to walk away.

"What's your name?" I called out before she disappeared.

"Jennifer," she replied and was gone.

I was startled awake by a loud tearing sound followed by an earsplitting crash. A gust of cold air intruded into my little hideaway, so I went to investigate what had happened. Snow was falling through a large hole where the roof had been. Roof joists and planking had crushed the couch where I'd been sleeping only three hours earlier.

Fire crews and police arrived a short time later. I relayed my tale of woe and told them they should search for the young lady who saved my life.

When I gave them her name, one of the firemen commented, "Don't worry she's fine."

I looked confused, and so he explained. "When the building first opened, a car rental clerk was killed in a freak accident. Ever since then, people have reported an attractive young lady offering them help. Her name is Jennifer."

I had never believed in ghosts, but that's the thing about beliefs, they are always subject to change.

Mark A. Gagnon

Just Enough Time

When Cher sang "If I Could Turn Back Time," she had no idea that I had been doing that and much more for several years. Time was never my friend, or so I thought, until the day of my accident. It was one of those freak occurrences that I would laugh about if it had happened to someone else. I was on a tropical vacation, enjoying the surf and sand, when a gust of wind dislodged a coconut from its perch high in a palm tree, and it hit me square on the forehead. I know, hilarious right, like something out of a fifties cartoon. As a result of the accident, I was in a coma for three weeks.

I finally came to with a splitting headache, surrounded by beeping machines. As I struggled to regain my equilibrium, I upended a tray with a drink on it. As the glass began to tumble from the tray, the first word to pop into my mind was *STOP*, which is precisely what the glass did. It just hung in mid-fall, defying gravity. My immediate reaction was to dismiss what I was experiencing as an effect of a muddled mind, and that reality would take over shortly, letting the glass hit the floor. The glass continued to hang in space until I grabbed it, and using a swooping motion, put the liquid back in the container as I replaced it on the tray. My next thought was *that's better*, and the sounds in the room resumed.

I left the hospital several days later, not mentioning the incident to anyone. I wanted to experiment with my newfound superpower, but first, I needed more information. At the local library, I read up on time travel and time manipulation. Of course, everything I read was theoretical, but one theory caught my attention— the Butterfly Effect. If a butterfly flaps it's wings on one side of the planet, the disturbance may cause a major event on the opposite side of the globe. A brief suspension in time to rescue a falling glass may have an insignificant effect, or it could cause an auto accident in a different part of the world because the flow of time was interrupted. Definitely nothing to use as a party trick.

I left the library playing out different scenarios in my mind that would justify using my new power. Ironically, it was while I was deliberating the question that a small child broke away from her mother and ran into the path of an oncoming truck. *STOP* I shouted in my mind, and all activity froze. I walked to the girl, picked her up, and returned her to her mother, placing the girl's hand into her mother's, then I thought the word *GO*. All motion returned to normal with the truck passing the mother and child without incident.

The Butterfly Effect could mean that the girl would later grow up to become the next Albert Einstein or the next Jeffry Dommer. No way to tell. What I knew for certain was I saved a life, and that can't be bad.

Mark A. Gagnon

XXI

Humans, look at them, each involved in their own little world; oblivious to everything around them, including me. I was human once, but I've evolved into something more, superior to what I once was. Now I look at these creatures as a wolf looks at a rabbit, or a cheetah at a gazelle; they are nothing more than prey. My quarry has unwittingly wandered within the boundaries of my hunting ground at the end of Canal Street. The elevated railway casts a perpetual shadow onto the pedestrian walkway below, obscuring sunlight during the day and blocking the glow from the city's lights at night; it's a predator's paradise. Now I must choose my evening's entertainment.

This will be the twenty-first time since my rebirth that I have selected a human for my personal fulfillment. Tonight's diverse candidates include: a homeless man tending to the plastic bags that contain all his worldly possessions; a female in her twenties walking briskly, skirt pushed up beyond mid-thigh by a playful breeze; two street musicians trying to earn a meager wage by playing to passersby; and an average guy walking his yip-yip dog. All are the unwitting participants in a contest to become my next and final trophy in this city.

Twenty-one will be the final entry in Volume I, a catalog chronicling my accomplishments. From here I will move on to a new city and state where I will begin Volume II. Each volume will have twenty-one chapters. Once I complete twenty-one volumes, I will publish them so the world can see what a truly evolved being can accomplish. Much has to be completed before I can attain my ultimate goal, starting with tonight's choice.

The homeless man is the easiest target. All I need to do is offer him a little money, maybe some food or booze, and he will follow me to his doom. Not a particularly satisfying final chapter.

The girl presents a higher degree of difficulty, but not the most difficult. I would need to attract her attention without creating an atmosphere of fear. She must see me as harmless, a wounded bird in need of care. Yes, more difficult than the homeless man and physically much more pleasurable.

Regarding the two musicians, I have never attempted a two-for-one before, but it's this type of challenge that starts my pulse racing. Maybe after listening to them for a while, I could suggest that a nearby party needs some live entertainment. The partygoers would surely pay to listen to such an accomplished duo. Logistics could be a significant problem. Two bodies are difficult to transport unless they are dismembered, and that's quite messy.

The most challenging of all is the guy with the dog. He looks to be in better than average condition, but not a match for a superior being such as me. The real problem is that damn dog. It's not large enough to do me harm; one swift kick, and the creature is out of the picture. No, it's the alarm the mutt will sound by yapping incessantly. If I had more time, I'm sure I would find a solution to this problem, but time is not my friend.

Today is a special day. Not only is it the twenty-first of the month but it's also the first day of a new moon. Humans are enamored by a full moon, but it's the new moon that has special powers, especially when it occurs on the twenty-first. Twenty-one, according to numerology, is a potent number because it is made up of three sevens, very powerful indeed. So, tonight when the clock strikes 21:21 I will add the twenty-first and last chapter to Volume I.

No time left for deliberation. My pulse quickens, eyes dart around scanning the area for anything that could thwart my plan. I make my selection as the minute hand rests on the twenty-first minute of the twenty-first hour. Time to act!

Who did I select to grace the pages of chapter twenty-one you ask? Fair question, and you'll be able to find the answer in the morning paper. Now it's time to fulfill my Destiny!

Printed in Great Britain
by Amazon